Dear Parent:
Your child's love of .... *here!*

Every child learns to read in a different way and at his or her own speed. Some go back and forth between reading levels and read favorite books again and again. Others read through each level in order. You can help your young reader improve and become more confident by encouraging his or her own interests and abilities. From books your child reads with you to the first books he or she reads alone, there are I Can Read Books for every stage of reading:

SHARED READING
Basic language, word repetition, and whimsical illustrations, ideal for sharing with your emergent reader

BEGINNING READING
Short sentences, familiar words, and simple concepts for children eager to read on their own

READING WITH HELP
Engaging stories, longer sentences, and language play for developing readers

READING ALONE
Complex plots, challenging vocabulary, and high-interest topics for the independent reader

ADVANCED READING
Short paragraphs, chapters, and exciting themes for the perfect bridge to chapter books

I Can Read Books have introduced children to the joy of reading since 1957. Featuring award-winning authors and illustrators and a fabulous cast of beloved characters, I Can Read Books set the standard for beginning readers.

A lifetime of discovery begins with the magical words **"I Can Read!"**

Visit www.icanread.com for information
on enriching your child's reading experience.

I Can Read Book® is a trademark of HarperCollins Publishers.

Sid the Science Kid: I'm Not Afraid of the Dark!
™ & © 2011 The Jim Henson Company. JIM HENSON'S mark & logo, SID THE SCIENCE KID mark & logo, characters and
elements are trademarks of The Jim Henson Company.
All Rights Reserved. Printed in the United States of America.
No part of this book may be used or reproduced in any manner whatsoever without written permission except in the case of
brief quotations embodied in critical articles and reviews. For information address HarperCollins Children's Books, a division of
HarperCollins Publishers, 10 East 53rd Street, New York, NY 10022.
www.icanread.com

Library of Congress catalog card number: 2010933266
ISBN 978-0-06-185261-9

Typography by Rick Farley
13 14 LP/ WOR 10 9 8 7 6 5 4 3
❖
First Edition

I Can Read!™

BEGINNING READING **1**

Jim Henson's™

SID the Science KID™

I'm Not Afraid of the Dark!

by Cari Meister

HARPER

An Imprint of HarperCollinsPublishers

"Sid," said Mom.

"Time to wake up!"

Sid rubbed his eyes.

He looked out the window.

"It's still dark," said Sid.

"I'm scared of the dark."

Sid turned on a light.

"That's better," said Sid.

"Now I can see."

"I want to know," said Sid.

"What happens in the dark?"

"Good morning, Sid,"

said Dad.

"Are you sure it's morning?"

said Sid.

"Yes," said Dad.

"It's just very early."

"Sid," said Mom,

"why are you afraid of the dark?"

"I can't see what happens

in the dark," said Sid.

"Do you think things change

when you can't see them?" said Mom.

"Hmm," said Sid. "I don't know.

Maybe I can find out at school."

At school, Sid asked his friends,

"Are any of you afraid of the dark?"

"I am," said Gabriela.

"One time I was sleeping in a tent. There was something scary outside."

"What was it?" said Sid.

"It was a tree!" said Gabriela.

"It just looked scary in the dark."

"Once," said Gerald,

"I woke up

in the middle of the night.

The hallway was dark and scary."

"Did something get you?" asked Sid.

"Nope," said Gerald.

"I turned on the light.

It was just my hallway."

"Interesting," said Sid.

"Rug time!"

said Teacher Susie.

Gerald closed his eyes

and pretended to bump into things.

He sat down and opened his eyes.

"It's not dark anymore!" he said.

"Have you all been talking about the dark?" Teacher Susie said.

"Yes," said Gerald.

"I get scared when it's dark."

"The dark can seem scary,"

said Teacher Susie.

"But when you think

like a scientist, it's not so scary."

"Let's try something,"

said Teacher Susie.

"Look around the room.

Touch the things you see."

Gabriela saw blocks.

She touched them.

Sid saw the bookshelf.

He touched it.

"Now," said Teacher Susie.

"Close your eyes.

Pretend it's dark.

Touch the same thing

you saw when it wasn't dark."

Gabriela touched the blocks.

"I feel the blocks," said Gabriela.

Sid touched the bookshelf.

"I feel the books," said Sid.

"Okay," said Teacher Susie.

"Open your eyes."

"Hey!" said Sid.

"Everything is the same

when it's dark."

"Let's go explore darkness
in the Super Fab Lab!"
said Teacher Susie.
"We are going to make
our own Cave of Darkness."

"I see," said Gabriela.

"We're going to use blankets!"

"That's right," said Teacher Susie.

"The blankets will block out
all the light."

"The cave might be scary," said Gerald.

"I will go in!" said May.

"Now," said Teacher Susie.

"I want everyone to draw what

it looks like in the cave."

"What do you see?" said Sid.

"I can't see anything," said May.

"It's really dark.

It's fun!"

"Cool!" said Sid.

After school, Sid had big news.

"I'm not scared of the dark
anymore," said Sid.

"How come?" said Dad.

"Today I learned that darkness just means there's no light," said Sid. "Things stay the same in the dark, so there's no reason to be scared!"

LAUGHTERNOON

a good time for some night jokes

Why didn't the chicken cross the road in the dark?

She was too chicken!

What kind of fish only comes out at night?

A starfish!

What did Sir Lancelot wear to bed?

A knight-gown!